Cal and the Amazing Anti-Gravity Machine

By the same author and illustrator

Violet and the Mean and Rotten Pirates

Cal and the Amazing Anti-Gravity Machine

Richard Hamilton

illustrated by

Sam Hearn

BLOOMSBURY CHILDREN'S BOOKS

First published in Great Britain in 2005 by Bloomsbury Publishing Plc,
38 Soho Square, London, W1D 3HB

A CIP record of this book is available from the
British Library

ISBN 0 7475 7564 9
ISBN 13 9780747575641

Printed in Great Britain by Clays Ltd, St Ives plc

10 9 8 7 6 5 4 3 2 1

All papers used by Bloomsbury Publishing are natural, recyclable products
made from wood grown in well-managed forests. The manufacturing processes
conform to the environmental regulations of the country of origin.

For Sara, Daphné and James – R.H.

For Warwick, who gave me his eyes,
and Mark, who offered me his glasses, just in case.
Thank you both – S.H.

Chapter 1

Early one summer morning, as the sun slanted across the roofs of a little town, picking out steeples and chimney pots and TV aerials and glinting off the blue-green wings of a flock of starlings gathered in the park, there was a sudden

CACOPHANOUS

EAR SPLITTING

BUILDING-SHAKING

TEETH-SHATTERING

NOISE.

CHANG-CHANG-CHANG-EEEEEEEEEEEECCCCH!

The residents of Gribbens Road groaned and pulled the bedcovers over their heads.

'SUNDAY MORNING!' bellowed an incredulous Mr Barraclough, beneath two pillows and a duvet.

'It's six o'clock!' shrieked a tearful Mrs Barraclough into her mattress.

This was their new house. They had only been here for two months, and they had been woken up in the middle of the night, or in the early morning, seven times.

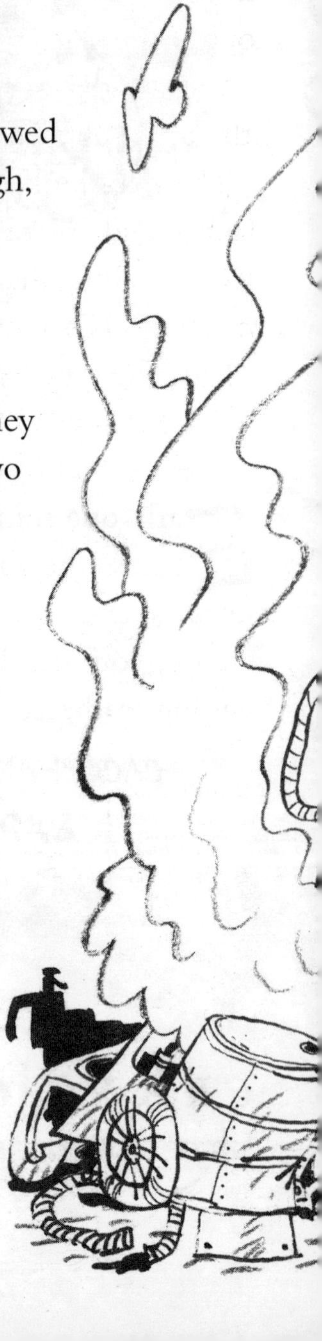

Their son, Cal, a quiet boy of ten, was in a room at the back of the house. He got out of bed and leaned out of his window. At the back of a neighbouring house, in a yard full of scrap metal, a man was operating a large piece of machinery. Smoke billowed from one end, sparks fired into the air from the other, and ribbons of shiny silver spiralled out of the side.

Cal wanted to shout at the man – but what was the point? A tidal wave of sound was filling the air.

The man looked like a giant fly. He was tall and lanky and wore oval-shaped goggles. He was feeding a long metal pole into the red mouth of the machine. His name was Frout. Mister Frout. He had long grey hair tied in a ponytail, and an oddly shaped beard that grew in a white wisp from his chin, like a dollop of Mr Whippy ice cream. He wore blue overalls and red braces and strong brown boots.

'Mr Frout!' Cal said to himself. 'Some of us are trying to sleep?' His voice went up at the end as if to say, 'didn't you know?'

His mother joined him. Only she took a more robust approach:

'Belt up you horrible, inconsiderate, thoughtless, idiotic, old CAVEMAN!' she screeched, and slammed the window down.

Cal looked at his mother. Mrs Barraclough's eyes were bloodshot and blazing, her unbrushed ginger hair stuck up on one side like a flaming bush. She closed her eyes and breathed in deeply. 'I'm sorry, darling,' she said loudly to Cal. 'I feel better for shouting, even if the selfish old buzzard can't hear me. Why, oh why, did we move here?' she groaned.

'What's he doing?' Cal asked, looking across to Mr Frout's garden.

His mother held up her arms and shrugged. 'I have no idea. The man is a menace. Just look at his garden. It's like living next to a shipyard. Mad Metal Monster Terrorises Neat Neighbourhood.' Cal's mother worked as a sub editor in a local magazine. She wrote headlines. Often she spoke in them too.

'Why can't he wait –'

'– until a decent hour?' his mother cut in. 'It is so inconsiderate. I shall talk to the council. I will raise it with the residents' committee. I shall contact the local TV. Anything to stop the torment.'

'C H A N G - C H A N G - C H A N G - EEEEEEEEEEEEEEEECCCCH!' spluttered the machine in Frout's yard.

There was a whining noise from under Cal's bed. It was their dog, Frankie. He had his paws cleverly held over his ears.

'This-is-driving-me-crazy,' sang the dog. Cal understood him, but his mother didn't.

'It's driving all of us crazy, Frankie,' Cal told him.

'Poor little thing,' Mrs Barraclough sympathised. 'You too are suffering.' She bent over and peered under the bed. 'And how did you get there, you naughty boy. Haven't I told you, Cal, the dog is not meant to spend the night in your bed. It's unhealthy.'

'He's not in my bed,' objected Cal.

'The dog has a basket in the kitchen. The kitchen door was shut,' said his mother.

'Maybe he let himself out.'

'Super Pooch Opens Doors with Paws. Come *on*.'

'The-dog-has-a-name,' complained the dog, in his gruff growling sort of way.

'He's definitely unhappy,' said Mrs Barraclough, frowning. 'Maybe I should video him and take it as evidence to the newsroom. Dog Numbed by Noise. Oh boy.' She held her head as if it was about to fall apart, and strode out of the room.

Cal looked back at Frout.

He was feeding more metal into his machine. His features locked in a grimace of effort. The iron pole looked heavy. Suddenly there was a change to the rhythm of the noise: a spluttering, a hiccoughing of the machine. And, to the intense relief of everyone in Gribbens Road, the infernal thing chugged, swallowed – and – stopped.

Dead.

Silence.

Beautiful, blissful,
roaring, soaring
silence.

Returned.

The residents of Gribbens Road sank back into their duvets and pillows and breathed deeply again, groping towards their lost slumber, trying to recapture their escaping dreams, as birdsong twittered again in the summer trees.

But Cal and Frankie were up. They had things to do.

Chapter 2

It was a month since Cal met Frankie the dog for the first time. It was a meeting he would never forget. Even if he lived to be a hundred years old.

Frankie arrived in a cardboard box with holes cut roughly in the top. He had been living with an American friend of Mrs Barraclough for almost seven years, but now the friend was moving abroad and couldn't take an old dog with her. Cal's parents thought that having a dog would be good for a solitary boy like Cal, and there was room in their new house. So Frankie came around in a box with 'New Zealand Apples' printed on the side and was plonked, unceremoniously, on the sitting-room floor.

'Here he is,' said the American friend. She was a mature lady with a small hill of golden hair and a smart brown leather suit. 'He's real nervous and real angry. So watch out.'

There was a short silence, which Cal eventually filled. 'Is he a Jack Russell?' he asked.

'That's right. A feisty little fella. He's a good dog – likes walking, eating and sleeping, like all of us.' The lady smiled.

Cal's mother came into the room with coffee.

'Oh, how kind – you bought apples!' she exclaimed.

'That's the dog,' corrected the lady.

'Oh. Is he in there?' Cal's mother put the coffee on the floor and bent down to the box.

Her friend opened up the side and a little face appeared. Frankie was white with brown eyes and a black patch across his snout. He had small soft ears that flopped forward like little folded handkerchiefs.

'Darling dog – he's sweeeeet,' Mrs Barraclough purred. She bent over to stroke him.

'Gettorrrf,' growled Frankie.

'No. He's savage,' Cal's mother corrected herself, quickly withdrawing her hand.

'No, no. He just grunts,' said the lady. 'Never was a dog that grunts and groans like Frankie. I reckon he's got stomach trouble. But take no notice. The vet says he's fine – just likes a moan, that's all.'

Suddenly a loud bark erupted from inside the box:

Cal couldn't believe his ears. Cal didn't believe his ears. It was impossible. He looked at his mother, then at the lady in leather. It flashed through his mind that she might be a ventriloquist, someone who could speak without moving their lips and 'throw' their voice to the other side of the room.

But both were behaving as if nothing had happened. They hadn't heard it. At least they hadn't heard words.

'Strange noise,' remarked Mrs Barraclough, frowning.

'That's his groaning,' said the lady.

With a roar, Frankie shot out of the box as if his backside was on fire. He vaulted the sofa, crashed into the table, somersaulted in mid-air, and fled into the dining room.

'Whoa!' cried the lady, standing up and, by mistake, kicking the coffee over. 'Whoops!' she whooped.

In the other room Frankie tore round and round the dining room table, upsetting two chairs, and then charging at the patio doors like a bull.

Unfortunately the patio doors were shut.

He bounced back from the glass with a bone-crunching thud.

'Oh boy!' cried the American lady. 'He sure is mad! Gee – I'm sorry Linda. I've messed up your lovely carpet.'

'That's fine,' said Mrs Barraclough. 'Dashing Dog Causes Coffee Chaos,' she smiled grimly, and hurried out to get a cloth.

Cal went into the dining room. He found Frankie hiding behind the curtain. The little dog was blinking. He looked confused and angry.

Cal noticed a row of sharp little teeth.

'Ah-hate-boxes,' snarled the dog, in a voice that had an odd American twang. 'And-windows,' he added, rubbing his nose in his paw.

Cal stared incredulously. The dog was talking. In a gruff, growly way, but unmistakeably talking.

Frankie looked up at Cal, narrowing his eyes.

'You-hearing-me?' he asked gruffly, speaking out of the side of his mouth.

Cal moved slowly to the other end of the patio doors and crouched down. He nodded to the dog. All the time he was looking into the dog's eyes. Imagine a friend, a real dog friend. He couldn't really believe what he had heard, but at the same time he was willing it, wishing it to be true.

'I hear you,' he said softly.

Frankie the dog looked at Cal the human carefully. His eyes took in every detail: boy, ten years old, messy, dressed in jeans and an old shirt. He had fair hair, a kind face. Big teeth. No threat, Frankie decided. Maybe, even, a friend? Frankie's tail twitched a little. It almost wagged.

Cal smiled encouragingly. Frankie relaxed and looked around the room. He looked through the patio doors out into the garden. He saw the big tree at the end, the shed and the other houses beyond. He saw a huge, bizarre metal construction, almost as high as a house, rising out of a neighbour's garden. What was that?

Then he took in the smells. The Barraclough smell (warm and a bit cheesy), the furniture

polish (a sharp lemon), the dust (dry), and beyond that, burned toast from breakfast, acrid coffee, grass, spilled ink, soap, diesel, grease and oil, and hot metal (strange) coming from that other garden …

At last the boy spoke.

'Hello.'

Frankie seemed to think. Then he said, or rather, growled, 'What's-yer-name?'

And from then on, Cal and Frankie were inseparable. They spent almost all their time together. Cal found that no one else understood Frankie. All they heard was a growly old dog with a rumbly tummy. But Cal heard about Frankie's life and his dreams and his favourite foods and his favourite walks and his favourite smells. And though he didn't really want to, he heard about all his aches and pains, and his digestion system too. For Frankie was getting on a bit in dog years – he was forty-nine – and his aches and pains and his digestive system were something of a concern to him.

Chapter 3

On the Sunday morning of the cacophonous, ear-splitting noise, Cal got dressed while his mother went back to bed. Frankie came out from hiding under the bed, and jumped up on a chair by the window.

'That man is noisy,' he grunted. 'That thing was so loud, it made my ears go funny. They're buzzing like bees. Your ears buzzin'?'

'No.'

'Maybe I should go to the vet?' Frankie mumbled. 'My hearing ain't what it used to be.'

'You could hear Mr Frout though?' Cal asked.

'They could hear Frout in Fiji!' replied Frankie. 'My teeth were almost shaken out of their sockets.

Maybe I should see a dentist?'

'I don't think dogs go to the dentist, do they?' asked Cal.

'They can in California!' said Frankie. 'Dentists, doctors, health farms, fitness centres. In California I could go shopping and have a bank account!'

'OK. But this is England. I don't think we have doggie bank accounts. Come on. Let's go and see what Frout is doing.'

They slipped downstairs, through the stale air in the kitchen, past a table still covered in glasses and plates from the night before, and into the back garden. It was quiet here and the air was cool. They crossed the dewy grass, leaving a trail of wet footprints. Frankie led the way, scampering this way and that, his nose sniffing urgently.

He stopped by a gap in the hedge and breathed deeply. 'Myrtle from no. 9,' he muttered. 'Out late again.'

'The cat?' asked Cal.

'Yeah,' said Frankie with longing. 'That cat is such a tease.' Frankie would have dearly loved to chase the cat, but he wondered what would happen if the cat got away. Oh, the humiliation! Frankie shuddered.

At the end of the garden they jumped on to the compost bin and then up on to the wall, and from there Cal lifted Frankie on to the roof of the shed. This was where they spied on Mr Frout. Flat on their fronts, like soldiers on a secret mission, they crawled up the roof.

'This makes my tummy tickle,' whispered Frankie, his whiskers twitching.

They got to their usual spot at the top and looked out across the path to the park that divided them, over to Frout's garden.

It was a hideous mess. In fact, it wasn't much of a garden, because hardly anything grew there. Nothing could grow there. From end to end lay piles of scrap metal.

There were iron girders and copper pipes, aluminium window frames, zinc taps and brass doorknobs. There were car parts and boat parts, train parts and plane parts. There were rusting anchors and propellers and radiators and big round oil drums.

Cal was fascinated by this scrapyard. He longed to go over and see inside. He couldn't believe so many things were made out of metal. There was so much metal that it had grown into two towers, almost as high as the house itself. Inside these towers were passages and platforms and ladders leading from one level to another. Mr Frout must

125

have spent years welding these towers together into this amazing sculpture of scrap metal. Cal often gazed at it trying to see where things came from. Was that big chute an air vent from a factory? Or a slide from a playground? Where did that Victorian fireplace come from? And who had sat in front of it when it was a fireplace?

'Where is he?' whispered Cal, scanning the yard.

'In the tower,' Frankie nodded to the tower nearest the park that the houses backed on to.

At that moment Mr Frout came out carrying a metal pole. His goggles were pushed to the top of his head and Cal could see his ice blue eyes, busy calculating. He took the pole to the middle of the yard and dropped it with a clang. Then he walked round and round the pole, drumming his fingers together.

'It's another experiment,' said Cal.

'Don't let him see you,' whispered Frankie.

Cal nodded. You could tell Mr Frout didn't like people. He gave the impression that he was far, far too busy to be bothered with other people. Cal's mother had waved a cheery 'Hello' when they first moved in, but Mr Frout had scowled

andlooked embarrassed. He might as well have stuck his tongue out.

It seemed that Mr Frout was some sort of inventor. He spent all his time doing experiments. Crazy, weird experiments. All day long there was sawing or banging or whizzing coming from the yard. Bits of metal would ping across the garden, or a machine would cough and splutter and roar. It was driving Cal's Mum and Dad mad.

But Cal didn't mind. He was drawn to the yard. It was noisy, but it was fascinating. It wasn't just another garden – something was happening over there, something he wanted to investigate.

Mr and Mrs Barraclough closed their eyes and blocked their ears – but Cal watched and listened and learned. And what he saw was amazing.

In the first week Frout had made a huge vacuum cleaner that could suck (with frightening force) the juice from a grapefruit or an orange. The juice shot down a glass tube into a glass on a table laid for breakfast.

Then Frout invented a very noisy and complicated machine that seemed to be designed to build brick walls (but which didn't. Instead it piled bricks and spat cement at them.)

Next he tried to make a firework that exploded with fruit (the idea was beautiful but the reality was rather messy, as bits of banana and orange and apple burst in mid-air and landed all over the gardens of Gribbens Road.)

The following week he built a 'hot-water-bottle bed'. It was like sleeping on a radiator (so very warm) but, when Cal saw Frout in the morning, he was pink and lightly cooked.

Every so often Frout noticed the boy peering at him from his bedroom window or from the top of the shed. He wished he wouldn't. He didn't like children. He thought children were a nuisance.

This is how he thought: children get under your feet and trip you up. They ask irritating questions. They fiddle with things. And they need looking after!

Mr Frout's sister had children. Four whining, whingeing, weedling little brats, he thought. They had to be fed. They had to be bathed. They had to be dressed. They had to be told how to behave – not once, not twice, but hundreds of times! When Mr Frout's sister came to visit (she only ever came once), she told her children not to touch anything.

'Don't touch,' she said. 'Don't touch.' Then she said it again and again and again until she'd said it eight hundred times. Frout was cross-eyed with irritation, practically exploding with madness: the children wouldn't listen. They touched. Everything. All the time. They fiddled and poked and prodded all his things. Bah! Children!

And as for that boy who watched him across the path – he even had a dog! (Don't get him started on dogs!) And together they were watching him right now! On top of that shed.

'Don't let him see you,' said Frankie again, keeping his snout below the edge of the roof.

'Hey! Look at that!' exclaimed Cal, under his breath. 'That is the biggest magnet I have ever seen.'

High in the air, Frout was hoisting an enormous horseshoe magnet. He secured it and then wheeled another into position below. Two more, one on each side, completed the preparations.

'That man's magnet-mad,' muttered Frankie.

Now Frout took the pole he had been feeding into the noisy machine earlier in the morning, climbed a stepladder, and placed it in between the magnets. It hovered in the air. It was two metres up, held by the magnetic force. Mr Frout walked round and round it. He admired it.

Then he snapped his fingers and lifted his foot as if he was about to dance. But that wouldn't do. He didn't dance. Even when he had had a great idea.

Chapter 4

'I never went to dog school, so how do I know what it is?' complained Frankie.

'I'm trying to tell you,' Cal persisted. 'Magnetism is a force that runs through the earth up to the north pole and down to the south pole and affects metals.'

It was later in the morning and they were once again lying on top of the shed roof. The beech tree above shaded them from the hot sun. Frankie was panting. Mr Frout had disappeared inside the towers for several hours. Cal and Frankie had had breakfast, had gone for a walk in the park, and had returned to Frout-Watch.

'Can you see magnetism?' asked Frankie, between pants.

'No. But you can't see the wind,' replied Cal, not sure whether this was helpful. 'It's the same force that attracts the magnets to the fridge – you know the letters and things that Mum sticks to the fridge?'

'I got you,' said Frankie. 'So the big pole was held in the air by magnet force. What next?'

Cal didn't need to answer – for at that exact moment there was a loud clanking sound from Frout's yard. They looked up and were confronted by a strange sight.

Out of the house strode a tall figure dressed in a shining suit of armour. It had to be Frout.

'Hey, cool. A medieval knight!'

'What's a medieval knight?' Frankie asked, suspiciously.

'Hundreds of years ago, warriors would wear armour like that in battles to protect them from all the arrows and the swords.'

'Yeah?' Frankie frowned. His tongue was hanging out. He shook his head. 'Must be hot in there! Good thing he's got that gap in the front to stick his tongue out!'

They watched as Frout gathered up some wires, and then climbed a stepladder to where the metal pole had been. He reached the top of the stepladder and pulled the wires. There was the distinct click of a switch.

A gentle humming began.

'What's that?' demanded Frankie, his little ears skewering towards the sound.

'I don't know,' said Cal, tiring of the questions. 'Wait and see.'

Slowly, and very carefully, Mr Frout, still holding the wires, jumped off the stepladder into thin air. The stepladder toppled over with a crash.

'Holy dog biscuits, big bones of bison!' Frankie stopped panting.

'Wow!' Cal breathed.

Frout was hovering in the air.

'He's going up!' Cal squeaked.

And he was. Frout was rising, very slowly, into the air. The humming was growing louder. Slowly his arms and legs splayed out and he hovered in a star position, a full three metres above the ground. On his face there was a terrified grin.

But something surprised Frout. The suit of armour had a helmet with a visor – a metal grill on a hinge that could cover the face to protect it – and until now, the visor had been open. Only now it snapped shut.

Everything happened at once. There was a muffled yelp as Frout's beard was caught in the helmet, like a brush trapped in a door. He jerked his arms about, trying to push the visor up again, but in doing so, he let go of the wires. He immediately began to shoot up and down and then spin, as if he was stuck in a washing machine. 'Uh-Uh-Uh-Uh-Uh,' he grunted.

After a short cycle, he stopped spinning and was left dangling upside down. Now he looked like a medieval knight who had been thrown out of a castle window and was frozen in midair.

The visor was open and a panting red face visible.

'Uh,' he said again.

Frankie was laughing. It was a kind of snigger – air squeaked and whistled through his nostrils, and his little paws kicked in the air. 'Eeeeh. Eeeeh. Eeeeh.'

'Shhh,' Cal said. 'I don't think that was meant to happen. He's in trouble.'

'He sure is,' squeaked Frankie. 'That's the dumbest thing I've seen all year.'

Frout was hanging dangerously high in the air. Now he had let go of the wires, he was stuck.

He looked at the sky, the roofs, the houses and the trees in the summer sunshine. He looked at the wires down below that had boosted the force with an electrical current. He needed them. Now. But how?

And then he saw the boy.

'Uh. Help. Help me, would you?' he called, in a weak voice. 'Now – I … I need the wires.'

Cal and Frankie looked at each other. Should they? Help the Mad Metal Monster? Cal didn't hesitate, this was his chance. As he climbed down from the shed, he wondered what his mother would say, but then she always said that he should help people who were in trouble, didn't she?

Chapter 5

Mr Frout reviewed his situation. He was three metres above the ground, upside down, in a suit of armour, on a stifling hot day. He was held there by a magnetic force, boosted by a humming core of electricity. This was exciting. Uncomfortable. And now he thought about it, dangerous too.

Worse, he had to get a boy to help him! A boy!

Right, well, maybe boys were useful for some things.

'Are these the wires?' Cal asked, below him picking up two wires leading to a dangerous machine.

He would have to speak to the boy. 'That's right. Pass them up, lad.'

Cal tried to reach. He moved the stepladder and climbed up. But he couldn't reach. Frout had risen and was now too high.

'I don't think I can do it,' Cal told him.

'Try pulling a wire,' barked Frankie, who had decided it was wise to stay clear and sit on the wall.

Cal climbed down the stepladder. He looked up at Mr Frout. The wires ran to a machine on the ground.

'Don't touch!' growled Mr Frout, as if reading Cal's mind. 'I know little boys – they touch. Touch bloomin' everything! This experiment is delicate. Pull the wrong wire and I'll shoot towards the ground like a ballistic missile!'

'How about you just give it a little tug?' suggested Frankie.

'A little tug?' asked Cal.

'A tug?' Frout yelped. 'Eh … ' he tried to think. What choice did he have? It was so hot. He was steaming in this heavy armour. Like being a cauliflower in a pressure cooker. 'Right. But mind you're careful. Give the left hand one a tweak. A little tweak mind! This machine

might be quite sensitive.'

Cal held his breath and tweaked. Nothing happened. He pulled a little harder. He tugged. Still nothing. So he gave the wire a big heave. Above him there was a shriek. Frout shot up.

'Other one!' He screamed as he banged his head on the huge magnet above him. 'Orrrrrrrr!' he groaned.

Cal pulled the other one. Hard.

Frout flew back. 'Ahhhhh!'

Miraculously, he stopped half a metre above the ground.

'STOP! Don't touch,' he gasped. His eyes were popping out of his red face. He held out his hands. 'Give,' he pleaded.

Cal gave him the wires, carefully.

Mr Frout tweaked, very gently, very precisely, on

both wires. It was as if he was flying a very sensitive kite. There was a click and the humming stopped, the machine slowed, and Frout sank with a gentle crumple of armour, on to the ground.

'Back to earth,' he said weakly, imagining perhaps that he was a returning astronaut. He looked up at Cal. His face twitched for a few moments and he managed to mutter, 'Thanks, lad.'

'That's OK,' said Cal lightly. He looked around at the yard. He felt small in amongst the piles of hard strong metal. The towers cut out the sun and the air tasted of oil.

Frout was struggling to remove his helmet. He pulled and pushed and twisted. Cal wanted to help, and felt he ought to, but wasn't sure how. Frout began to curse about rotten, useless, medieval armourers. About idiotic, stupid designs. About shoddy workmanship.

Then he stood and clasped the helmet in both hands and pulled. He let out an enormous grunt, jumped in the air, and sat down again.

'Can … can I help?' Cal managed to say.

Frout turned his icy blue eyes on him: *You? Help?* they seemed to say.

'Tell him there's a buckle on the side,' Frankie spoke from the wall.

'There's a buckle on the side,' Cal told Mr Frout.

'Ah! I might have been stuck in that for weeks,' he said, as the helmet came off. His hair was stuck to his forehead, his face was pink and glistening.

'You could have been stuck in the air too,' Cal told him.

'Yes,' Frout nodded. 'I could.' He frowned and

rubbed his brow and looked suddenly deep in thought. Then he brightened. His face creased, and he actually smiled. He looked at Cal, looked him up and down, as if he was seeing him for the first time. 'Experimentation! You've got to experiment and you've got to take risks. That's what I say. Now, I'd better go and change,' he said abruptly, and clankedoff towards the house.

Cal looked at Frankie lying in the sun on the wall. Frankie opened an eye. 'We got one here,' he muttered.

'He's not so bad,' Cal spoke softly.

'Whaddayamean? He's a fruitcake,' said Frankie.

Cal looked around the yard. He relaxed. He was struck by how many things were ordered here. There was a bank of little boxes all neatly labelled. Shelves with jars of nails and screws and hooks. On the ground floor of the tower, there were tools hanging up, carefully arranged. It looked like a great big messy scrapyard from a distance – but in

fact it was surprisingly ordered, when you looked closely.

'Hello again,' Mr Frout reappeared at the back door in his overalls and red braces. Cal noticed how he waved his arms around nervously when he talked.

'As I was changing just now, I, er, had an interesting idea. I'm not used to having guests but …' (and here his arms waved in a circle) 'how would you like to try the world's first Pneumatic Milkshake?'

Cal smiled. Any milkshake was OK by him, even a –

'Pneumatic,' Frout repeated. 'Spelt with a silent P. It's compressed air. Like the air you put in a bicycle tyre. I keep it all over the place. And just now it struck me that, if I blast milk, banana and honey in a force 12 hurricane of compressed air, it could be, like, tasty?'

'Will it be full of air?' asked Cal.

'Maybe. Maybe light as a cloud.'

Mr Frout went inside and fetched an enormous glass jar and some milk and bananas and honey. He poured the ingredients into the jar and fixed a sturdy rubber plug into one end. He fiddled about for a bit, clamping the glass jar into place, and fetching a wiggly pipe, which he fixed into the plug.

'Take cover,' he advised. 'It's possible the glass jar will explode, despite its toughened status.'

Frankie scampered to the end of the wall. Cal took cover behind a car door. Frout strode up and down, checking things and rechecking them. He was absorbed in his work. At last he retreated himself, put on some goggles and flicked a switch.

There was a terrific *whoosh* and the jar turned white with milk, as the contents were blasted with the compressed air. After thirty seconds, Frout turned off the air.

'Come on,' he waved to Cal. 'I have a good feeling about this one.' He strode over, rubbing his hands.

They took the lid off the jar and peered inside. There was a glorious yellow froth and a fine, bananary smell wafted up. Frout tried to tip the contents into a cup. Only the froth stuck there.

'It's all froth!' Cal grinned. 'Banana froth!'

'Hey! That's a first!' cried Frout delightedly. 'I'll fetch some spoons.'

He went off and returned with three spoons and they tucked into the world's first Banana Froth. It was delicious (though it did have a tendency to make them burp!). It struck Cal how generous it was of Frout to include Frankie. They took a spoonful over to him on the wall. Cal decided he quite liked Frout. It was surprising how quickly one could make friends. How wrong you could be about somebody.

Mr Frout was thinking something similar. How wrong he had been to think that all children were irritating brats. This one was rather good company. Not only that – he was clever. He looked the reliable sort. In fact, thought Frout, he would make an excellent assistant.

Chapter 6

'You what?' asked Mrs Barraclough. 'You did what?' Sometimes there seemed no halfway mark on the dial of Mrs Barraclough's temper. She went from zero to ten in a second.

'He was stuck and I helped him, and then we talked, and he's really quite nice.'

'But you don't know him!'

'Yes, I do. He's a neighbour.'

'A neighbour doesn't mean that you know them! Haven't I taught you anything?'

Cal was silent. His mother was silent. Cal tried a different approach. He softened his voice. 'I'm sorry, Mum. He needed help. And he really was nice.'

'Ah.' His mother was cooling down. 'That's something, then. Nasty Neighbour Turns Nice.' Luckily Cal's father called at that moment and Mrs Barraclough was distracted. Cal slipped into the garden and made himself scarce.

For the next week Cal and Frankie watched Mr Frout and his experiments. Cal waved to him, but didn't go over. He tried to think of some of his own experiments, and started a notebook with diagrams of his inventions. Drawing them was fun. Actually making them might prove more tricky.

He started with some small things:

A vacuum cleaner that sorted the things it sucked up into different sections – dust, small toys, jewellery.

Then he invented an 'Umbrella-Walking Stick-Stool-Sword-Torch-Ladder' all combined.

He designed a mobile phone that combined a handwarmer, an electric whisk and a secret pack of playing cards.

His favourite design was the very ambitious, and complicated, 'Getting-Dressed-and-Eating-Breakfast-while-Watching-TV-and-Finishing-Homework-Machine'. It did everything for you.

His second favourite was the 'Washbasin Assistant' that would clean teeth, wash face and hands, and dry you, without you having to lift a finger.

And, for Frankie, there was a 'Doggie Exerciser', complete with a cat to chase, sticks and balls to catch, and a bone to dig for – all in the comfort of your own home, and taking up a minimum of space.

Cal wondered if he should show them to Mr Frout.

Mr Frout, meanwhile, was busy with his own designs. He was arranging magnets and mirrors and a huge rubber band, that spun round and made sparks of electricity fly from a large silver sphere.

One evening, when the air was very still, Cal noticed Frout's yard covered in fog. It was extraordinary because nowhere else was foggy. There was a new chugging noise, too, interspersed by cracks.

'Mr Frout!' called Cal, from the top of the shed, when he was unable to contain his curiosity any longer.

Frout's head popped out of the blanket of fog.

'What are you doing?'

'Hello, lad. Yes. Everything's fine,' he said, and disappeared.

It was an unsatisfactory answer, but Cal let it be.

'He's what you call unsociable,' Frankie gabbled, chewing on a stick. 'He don't like society. You know – people, dogs, that sort of thing. He's a guy who likes to be on his own. Secretive type.'

'I suppose hiding under a cloud is sort of secretive,' Cal agreed.

'It sure is pretty, the way it just sits there,' drooled Frankie, dropping the wet stick for a moment. 'Maybe when the sun goes down, it'll go all pink.'

'Come on,' said Cal. 'Let's go over. We can say we were worried about him. Mum's working upstairs. She won't know.'

As they jumped down from the shed, and clambered over the wall on to the ground that separated the gardens, a flash lit up the fog in Frout's yard. It was like lightening in a cloud.

'Cal,' said Frankie, in a guarded tone, 'I ain't so sure it's such a good idea to go in there.'

Cal paused. 'OK. We'll call.'

He ran over to the wall and scrambled up until he could lean his arms on the top.

'Mr Frout? Are you OK?' he called into the fog.

'Yes,' called a breathless and excited voice. 'It's pretty lively in here. It's amazing, amazing. I think I'm on the verge of something big. Something enormous … enormously big.' His face rose out of the fog. He was grinning. Cal noticed his big teeth and the beard, now split into two thin ice cream squiggles. He found Frout's excitement a little alarming.

'I am finding a very strange force at work,' Frout confided breathlessly. 'It is as if, as if, as if … as if I had got rid of, of, of, of gravity,' he gabbled. 'Things are lighter, somehow. Heavy things are light and light things are … floating.'

Cal frowned. Frankie coughed. It all seemed a little unlikely.

'If only …' Frout went on, jabbering, 'I could … could…' His voice trailed away. He looked at Cal and then at Frankie. Suddenly his eyes grew as he looked at the dog.

'I wonder,' he said conspiratorially. 'Would it be a good idea, I mean, if we, he, the dog there, he ...'

Whatever it was, Cal thought, was probably *not* a good idea.

Frout tried again. 'If I have found a new force – the opposite of gravity – then I need to test it, not just on metal and wood but flesh, to see if it would work for us. And maybe if I could put your dog ...'

'NO WAY!' shouted Frankie, and sat down firmly in the path. 'You cannot expect ME to be up for animal experimentation! I am against it! Obviously! If you're so keen on experimenting, YOU do it!'

Cal looked at Frout – but Frout read his expression. He held up his hands. 'Aye. What am I thinking? You're right. It's a terrible idea. Poor little mutt.'

'Why don't you do it?' suggested Cal.

'Well – yes, but I need help. I can't operate the machine and be the subject of the experiment at the same time.'

'I can help?' Cal asked.

Frout beamed. 'Will you? Yes. Thank you. Come over.' And he disappeared.

Cal dropped down to the ground. 'Are you coming?' he asked Frankie.

'No,' said Frankie. 'I am not. I'll wait for you here.' He stuck his snout in the air, independent and offended.

'OK, that's cool.' Cal climbed the wall and dropped into the fog on the other side.

The fog was thick and very cold. Cal wished he had a jumper on. He held out his hands and walked forward carefully. 'Hello!' he called.

'Over here,' Frout's voice came out of the fog. Cal found him crouching down fiddling with a set of levers. he looked like a wizard, ancient and mystical.

'Take hold of these levers here, they've got little lights on top. See? Green for go, red for stop. Blue

controls the magnetic and static electrical mix.'

'How does it work?' asked Cal.

There was a long pause.

Frout seemed to be battling with the answer.

'I … I don't know,' he said at last. 'I wish I did. It's something I can't explain, something to do with metal. It's as if there is a force here that has altered the magnetic force. Changed it into something that eliminates gravity! Wipes it out. It's just chance that I stumbled upon it – but I have, and … are you with me?'

'Not really,' said Cal, baffled.

'Well, think of it this way: everything in the universe has an opposite – black has white, light has dark, silence and noise … and, somehow or other, I seem to have found the opposite of gravity – which until now, has never had an opposite! There.' He stood up. 'Now, when I give the signal, pull the green up, then slowly ease the blue up. I'll be over here and see if I can feel the power.'

'OK,' said Cal. He watched Frout disappear into the fog.

'Pull!' called Frout from across the yard.

Cal pulled. A hum pulsed around them and then a bolt of lightening crackled past, making Cal jump.

'The blue!' cried Frout excitedly.

Cal searched for the blue light. He was feeling a bit funny. He found the blue lever and pushed it up.

Immediately a double bolt of lightening shot past him and a vibrating hum swam dizzily around. Cal giggled. It was as if someone was tickling him. He felt all light and he heard Frout laughing too, across the garden, above him.

That was when he realised Frout was in the air. Above him. Floating. Which for some reason struck him as very funny indeed.

Then, through the laughter, he heard Frankie barking. 'Turn it off, Cal. Turn it off!' And he pushed the red lever, and the humming stopped, and the chugging of the fog machine died, and the lightning fizzed weakly. And the laughter in his head drained away.

There was silence.

'Unbelieveable,' squeaked Frout, away to Cal's left.

Cal went towards the voice. Frout was lying on the ground laughing.

'I was rising in the air. Astonishing!' he exclaimed. He gazed at Cal. 'The possibilities for this invention are huge!' he whispered, looking suddenly serious and madder than ever. 'Missiles! Missions to Mars! Giant vegetables! Oh Cal, thank you for your help. I must go immediately. I've got work to do.'

And he vanished into the fog.

Chapter 7

Frout disappeared for days. In the meantime, Cal thought about the loss of gravity. What would it mean? He looked in books and on the internet and tried to imagine what the world would be like if everything was weightless.

He thought of floating to school, of being able to kick a football several miles, of lifting something really heavy (like, say, a car) with just one hand! Life would be totally different.

'Keep your feet on the ground,' Frankie told him. 'I don't want to run a mile to fetch a football. Maybe you imagined it and Frout didn't float at all.'

But Cal disagreed. He remembered how he had felt

light, almost weightless, how it made him giggle with excitement. (Now that was strange. Why had it made him giggle?) What would his schoolmates say if he and Frout had discovered a force that was the opposite of gravity? You could win the Nobel prize for that! He imagined winning the Nobel prize. He could float down to collect it, make a speech about the trials of experimentation as he bobbed above the podium.

'I wish you were trying to invent the perfect dog basket,' Frankie told him. 'One with a water mattress and some bone-flavoured wicker to chew. And for the older dog, something special to calm the stomach after one of those indigestible biscuit meals you owners are so fond of.'

Cal laughed. 'I think one with a nice scratchy blanket with pongy dog smell all over it – a basket that could take you for a walk twice a day.'

'And didn't say "heel" all the time,' added Frankie.

'And would let you chase rabbits,' suggested Cal.

'That would take you where there were some rabbits to chase!' Frankie muttered, tucking his head between his paws and going flat. He closed his eyes. Time to dream.

As Frankie dreamed of perfect dog baskets and rabbits, Cal dreamed of returning to the machine Frout had made. He wanted to see what it was like to float.

But Frout was nowhere to be seen. He had been gone for two days. His metal yard was still. His house shut up. His rusty old truck had gone. Where was he?

'Hey, nice and quiet,' said Cal's father, raising his beer glass one evening when it was hot enough to sit outside.

'Barracloughs Bask in Balmy Bliss,' cooed Mrs Barraclough.

Cal slipped away to his room. It looked like his parents were about to get soppy. He opened the window to get rid of the stuffy air, and that's when he saw Frout.

He was wheeling a huge nest of copper wires into position, some more giant horseshoe-shaped magnets, and some mirrors. He was up to something. Cal watched as he arranged them all and dusk slowly fell.

'First thing in the morning, Frankie, we're going to go over and see him.'

'If you insist,' yawned Frankie, dozing on the bed. Cal looked at Frankie. How was it that dogs could doze and talk at the same time, he wondered. Frankie sighed, 'I'm not going in though. I don't want to be part of no experiment.'

But as Frankie trotted downstairs to his basket for the night, Cal thought to himself: *I do. I want to go in and be part of the experiment*. And he fell asleep thinking of that excitement, and practising asking Mr Frout if he could help.

But he woke too early, and it was still night. Watery moonlight filtered through the gap in the curtains. Cal got up to look out.

The first thing he saw was a thin layer of mist. His heart jumped. It was hanging eerily in the trees, lit by the bright moon.

Frout's yard was still. The metal towers rose out of

the mist, mirrors reflecting moonlight on to them. Frout wasn't there. Nothing was happening.

But Cal was wide awake. There was still an hour to go before dawn. He couldn't think about going back to bed now. He would go downstairs. Just to look again. Get into position early, ready for when Mr Frout came out. He wouldn't even wake Frankie.

He felt rather pleased with himself – he wasn't usually this adventurous.

He dressed and slipped downstairs, through the patio windows in the dining room so as not to disturb Frankie in the kitchen. He stole across the garden, silently. Everything looked different in the moonlight. The world was drained of colour. It felt spooky.

But when he got to the shed, he changed his mind about waiting. He wanted to take a closer look. So he climbed over the garden wall and across the path to Frout's yard. He climbed Frout's wall too, and looked. But he still couldn't see very well. He was so curious he could feel his fingers tingling. He was sure that Mr Frout wouldn't mind if he took an even closer look. So he jumped silently in.

Metal loomed around him – engine parts, wires,

pipes. More wires than ever. Seeing the lights of the level-crossing levers glowing like little fireflies, he went over to them and laid his hand on the green one.

This is the one Cal had pulled. His fingers closed around the lever. With his other hand he took hold of the blue lever. In the spirit of experimentation, he could … just … ease … it … a … little … bit …

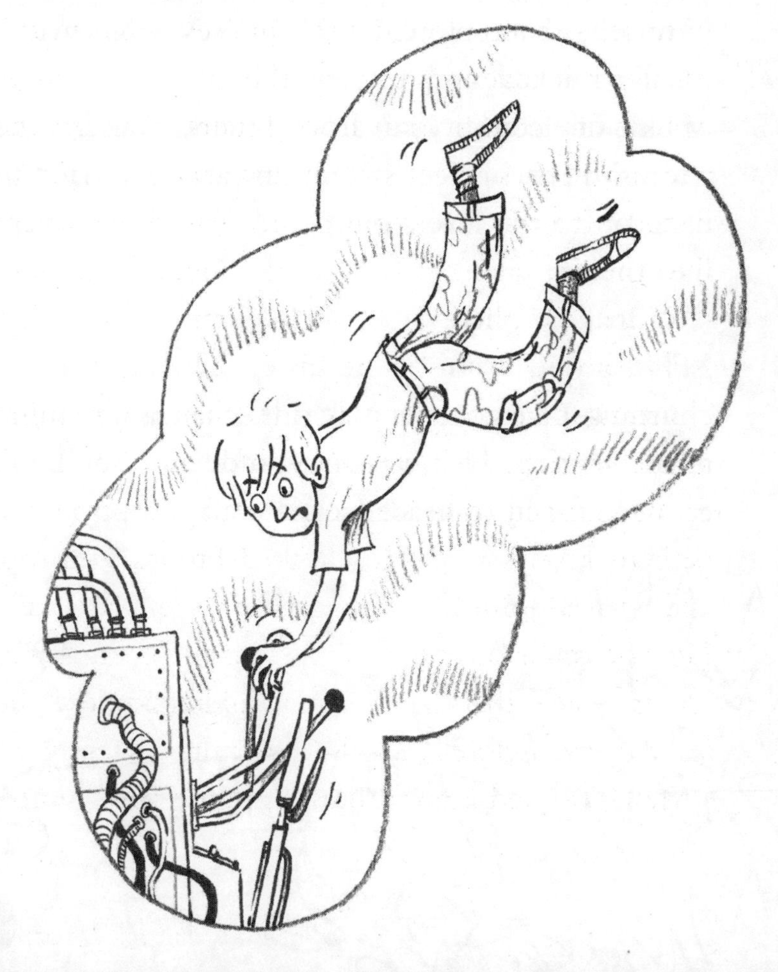

The lever swung forward abruptly, and a humming began. It was a deeper, more musical humming than before. UUUMMMMMMMMM.

Cal panicked and pushed the blue one up. A crackle of electricity ran around the yard and, to his astonishment, his feet swung upwards. He tried to hang on to the levers but couldn't, and was swept into the air.

'Whoa!' he cried.

Frout's yard swam before his eyes. It was stomach churning. Like a theme park ride. It felt as if it ought to be dangerous but, somehow, suddenly, Cal didn't care. He felt light-headed, carefree and happy.

Up we go! he thought. *Goodbye gravity! This is what it's like to be a spaceman.*

Hey! There was his bedroom! And the roof! He was looking at the roof. By the drainpipe. There was that tennis ball he'd lost last week, when he tried to hit it over the house.

Drifting down, here was the bathroom. He could push off the wall – *whooooosh!* – across to the beech tree. Cal sailed through the air, tumbling gently into the twigs and leaves.

Holding a branch to steady himself, he spat out a leaf that had got into his mouth, and paused. He looked down on the shed and his garden, seeing it all afresh, from a new angle. He felt light and happy. This was why humans wanted to fly. It was fantastic. It was the freedom, the fantastic freedom

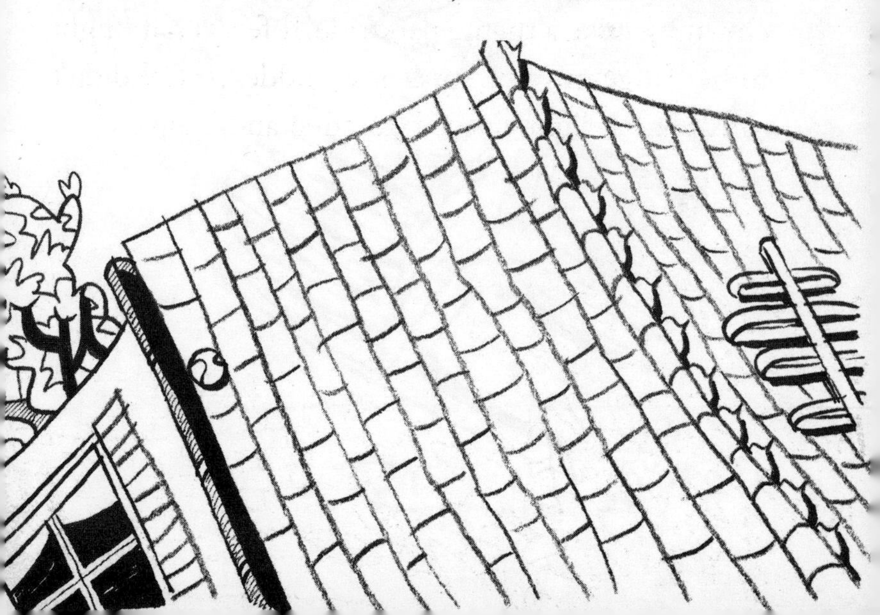

of space that was always around us and above us, but always out of reach. Only the birds could occupy it, darting through the air. How often had he wondered what it would be like to dive and swoop like a swallow? And now, here he was. He pushed off the tree into the air with his arms out like wings. Oh! This was beautiful.

He flew gracefully down to the garden near the back door. As he approached, he brushed a garden chair.

It tumbled over across the garden and began drifting up. Now, he noticed other things drifting too. The seat of his swing. His football. A flowerpot had fallen over and all its contents were floating across the lawn. Without gravity, nothing was held to the ground – things were breaking free.

Then he heard a growl in the kitchen. He pushed open the back door. His mouth fell open. A wave of food was hovering in the air. Pasta and biscuits and cereals. The fridge door was open, and a lettuce flew out. Cal swam over, through the food.

It was Frankie. He was deep in the fridge, rummaging.

'Frankie!' Cal exclaimed.

'Go away!'

'Frankie!' Cal said severely. A tomato slapped into his forehead.

Frankie stopped and turned around. He had guilt written all over his face. And beef stew.

'Go away! Please. I'm having the best dream of my life! I never got into the fridge before, this is heaven!'

'Frankie, it's not a dream. This is happening.'

'Get outta my dream,' Frankie warned. He bared his teeth at this threat to his enjoyment. 'And don't be dumb. I've had food dreams thousands of times. There's a chicken in here somewhere. It always ends with a big chicken …'

Cal grabbed him by the back legs and pulled him out. 'Look Frankie – does this happen in your dream? Does the food float everywhere?'

Frankie looked at the food floating through the kitchen and frowned.

'Proves it's a dream, man! That ain't reality!'

'But you can feel you're floating,' Cal said. To prove his point he pushed Frankie across the room.

'Whoa!'

But he'd forgotten his own strength. Without gravity, Frankie streaked across the kitchen, his eyes wide in surprise. He swept the jugs from the shelf above the cooker and bounced off the wall.

'Sorry!' cried Cal, reaching forward as Frankie came back like a pinball, nudging through assorted vegetables.

As the jugs hit the floor, they began to smash in slow motion. Shards of pottery began bouncing back into the air.

'Let's get out!' cried Cal. He took hold of Frankie by the collar, and pulled him out of the back door.

Chapter 8

Clasped in Cal's arms, Frankie blinked repeatedly. He looked left and right. Up and down. They were about a metre above the ground.

'Cal, is this Frout? Has he …?' whimpered Frankie. 'Is this the gravity thing?'

'Yes,' nodded Cal. He was staring out across the garden. A cat with legs splayed open and hair on end was flying across the yard. It looked as if it had leaped from a wall and continued to travel in the biggest jump it had ever made.

And then he saw the pond. It was moving. Large bubbles of water were rising up into the air. Cal pushed his way over and stared. It was extraordinary. Phenomenal. A bubble of water!

He prodded one bubble and little bubbles came off it. There were fish inside – swimming in a bubble of water.

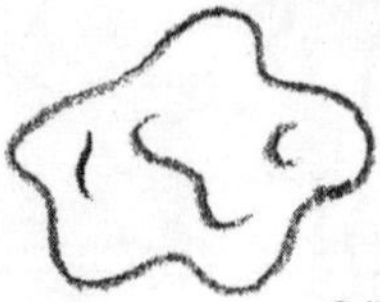

'You gotta stop this, Cal,' said Frankie sternly. 'This ain't just a bit of fun. This is serious. This has upset the natural order – terrible things could happen. My stomach is doing cartwheels.'

'It's amazing. And wonderful things could happen too,' said Cal, marvelling at everything around them. 'Think how we are squashed by gravity all the time. We could fly. We could float everywhere. There's a whole new world up here. Like Frout said, without gravity, plants would grow huge –

we could have tomatoes like footballs. Big bushes of broccoli! Everything would be bigger. Trees, people, dogs!'

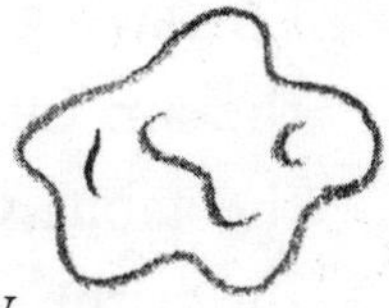

'I don't want to be bigger. I like being small!' exclaimed Frankie.

'And we could move things really easily. Without gravity, rockets could fly into space without using all that fuel. They could just push off the earth and they'd be there. We could explore the stars. You could go to the moon with a push. Just imagine.'

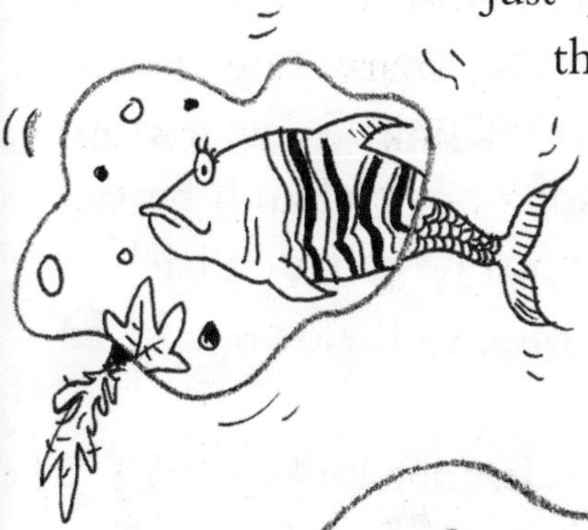

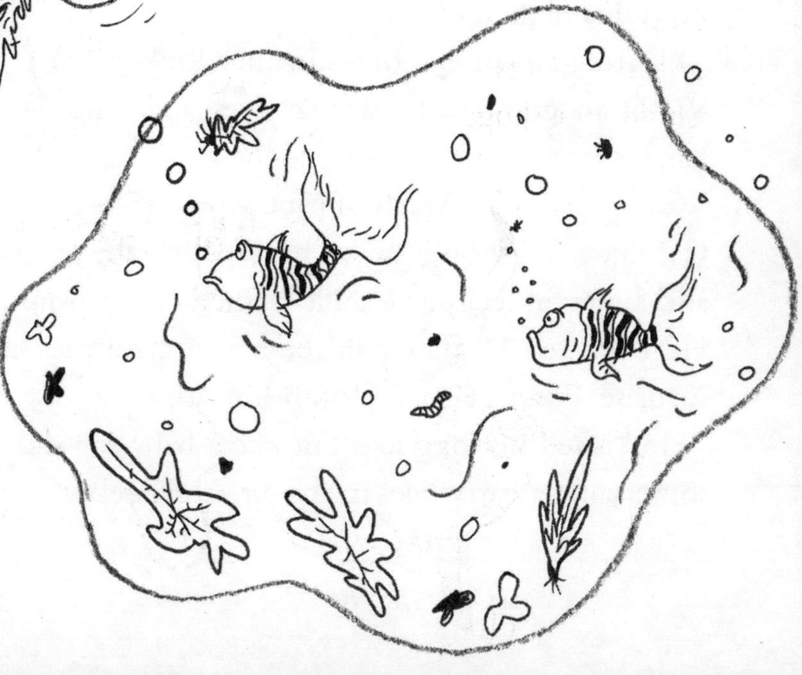

'So what?' Frankie barked. 'Imagine trying to eat your dinner with the food flying off your plate. Or having a bath with the water floating around in the air. Or playing cards when they won't stay on the table. Oh boy, what happens when you go to the bathroom? This is a recipe for chaos!'

But before Cal could reply, there were shouts from Frout's house.

Out of the upstairs window Frout came tumbling, head over heels. He looked as if he was having a fight with his dressing gown, as he tried to put it on. The arms wouldn't stay still and the top wouldn't come down, and first he had it on back to front, and then he had it on upside down, tangled up in his nightshirt.

Floating through the air, he looked like a Victorian ghost, with staring eyes and wild grey hair.

Cal stayed still. Maybe Frout wouldn't see him. Cal knew he should never have pulled the levers, and an awful feeling of guilt washed through him. He expected Frout would be furious. But, to his surprise, Frout began to laugh instead.

He kicked his long legs out like a baby. He did a somersault, a cartwheel in the air. A dance!

'Oh please,' muttered Frankie. 'I hate grown-ups dancing.'

'Mr Frout!' called Cal. Holding Frankie under his arm, he pushed off the ground and rose towards the inventor.

Frout beamed. 'Cal! This is astonishing!' he squealed. 'I feel like laughing, like singing, like jumping for joy. I'm flying! Come with me, lad.'

Frout grasped Cal's free hand and pushing off from the tower of metal, pulled them gently down towards the ground.

'We are in a bubble of zero gravity. Look at the way the trees and bushes are moving. It's as if they're under water. I feel light and free and strong. I could run a thousand miles! I could spit a thousand miles!' He picked up a heavy anchor with two fingers. 'Look: it's as light as a feather.' He grinned and blinked. 'Beautiful,' he sniffed.

Cal wondered for a moment if Frout was going to weep.

'Hello, dog,' he said to Frankie. 'You are the first dog to be in zero gravity on earth,' he told him. 'How do you like it?'

'The-dog-has-a-name,' growled Frankie.

'He's not sure,' said Cal.

'Oh. Well, it will take some getting used to, I reckon. Now, let's check out this machine.' Frout began examining wires and dials and mirrors and magnets. He was so excited, he could barely concentrate. He kept throwing his arms in the air and sighing, and shaking his head and laughing.

'Inside this bubble of zero gravity,' he explained to Cal, 'there is this house and your house and the gardens and a slice of the park. Beyond that, everything's normal. But,' his eyes glinted, 'imagine: what if the whole world was in zero gravity? Eh?'

'I don't know,' Cal replied. 'I think maybe, you know, that might be a little much?'

'Oh?' Frout twisted his beard round his forefinger. Cal saw how it got its distinct wavy pattern.

'Look, Mr Frout, the sun's coming up.'

Frankie barked. 'Hey. Look out guys!' he warned. 'Everyone's waking up.'

'Ouch!' Frout looked down. Something stung him.

At the same moment, Cal felt it too. 'Ow!' he rubbed his leg.

Suddenly the air began to fill with insects. Flies, bees, beetles, earwigs, greenfly, blackfly, moths and butterflies began to rise into the air in a crazy cloud. Everything that flew seemed to be changed and confused by the loss of gravity. They couldn't fly properly any more. Insects buzzed and fizzed and whined round and round.

'Ahhh. Yuk!' cried Frout, waving his arms around.

'Ugh!' Cal spat out a moth. Frout scratched his hair then grabbed his nightshirt at the bottom. 'Orrrr! They're swarming. Right up me shirt!' he cried.

'Gettorf!' yapped Frankie, kicking out and twitching his tail.

The insects flew in strange patterns, looping and zigzagging unnaturally.

'Look down!' cried Frankie. 'Snails!'

On the ground a carpet of slugs and snails were rising slowly. There were worms and beetles too.

'Everything's waking up, Mr Frout!' said Cal.

'Extraordinary! Remarkable! Disgusting!' cried Frout, fascination and horror written all over his face. He had flies in his hair and a butterfly buzzing in his nightshirt.

'Horrible. Vile. Bloomin' infestation!' he screamed, kicking out frantically.

A moment later some birds shot past them at high speed, and slammed into the metal towers. More followed. They were flying like bullets, only twisting and weaving out of control.

'Look out!' cried Cal. A duck shot past with a loud 'QUACK!' Feathers flew. A second later a pigeon hit Frout in the leg.

There was a shout from Cal's house.

'IMPOSSIBLE!'

It was Mr Barraclough. He opened the window in Cal's room and stared out. Behind him, Mrs Barraclough floated, screaming hysterically.

'IMPOSSIBLE!'

'Quick!' shouted Cal. 'Turn it off!'

'CAL!' cried his parents.

'I'm fine!' he called back, with a smile. He waved to his parents, hoping that if he pretended everything was quite normal, then they might think it was. A fox spun past.

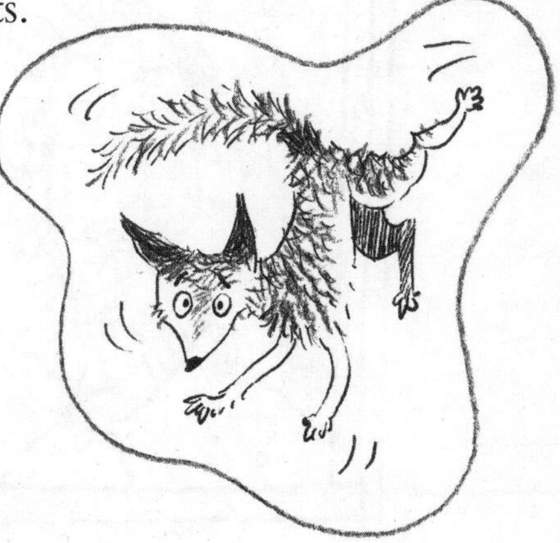

Cal shrugged in a 'Well, what-d'ya-know?' kind of way.

But it was pointless. He couldn't ignore the horrified look on his parents' faces. There was no point in pretending. Everything they could see was distinctly abnormal.

He let go of Frankie near the ground, and struggled over the wall to reach the machine. Small animals and insects wriggled around him. They were so itchy! Frout was squirming about, swatting insects and fending off floating debris like a madman.

'Turn it off!' Frout cried.

Cal found the levers and pulled. The humming changed. There was a high-pitched screech and a hideous sucking sound. Suddenly, Cal felt himself thrown away from the machine by a terrific force. He flew across the path between the gardens, into the branches of the beech tree.

The air cleared. *Zing!* Gone. Everything floating in the air had gone. Where?

It took several moments for him to realise what had happened. Cal looked up. The insects were above them in the sky. He hung on tightly to a branch.

I'm hanging on, he thought. I am looking up at the ground, but I feel like I am going to fall into the sky. He looked down to his feet. Past his feet lay the sky. He felt he was being sucked into the sky.

'Are we back to normal?' he heard Frankie ask from his position under a bush on the ground.

'Not exactly,' Cal whispered. 'In fact, not at all.'

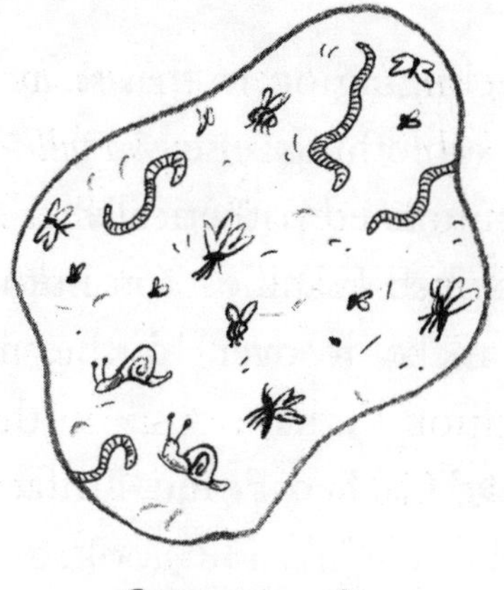

Chapter 9

They were upside down. Instead of everything falling back to the ground, it had all fallen into the sky.

Frout was hanging on to a small tree by the wall.

'Disaster. Total disaster,' he panted. 'The force field has changed. We have moved from zero gravity to *anti*-gravity. This is big trouble!'

'Turn-it-off,' growled Frankie. He seemed to be hanging on to something by his teeth.

'Can't you turn it off?' echoed Cal to Frout.

'I'm …' Frout began. He looked suddenly lost, unsure. 'I can't. I'm stuck,' he said, lamely. Cal looked from the beech tree to the ground. He saw Frout's sagging shoulders, his long wild grey hair, how he was clinging on in that shambolic dressing gown. And something else. Fear? 'What have I done?' Frout moaned pathetically.

'Oh boy!' sighed Frankie. 'You humans!'

'Can you make it over to the machine?' Cal asked.

'I can't move,' sobbed Frout. 'I'm terrified.'

Great, thought Cal. He looked over to the machine in Frout's yard. It was making a high-pitched humming noise. Someone, somehow, had to turn it off. If he could get to it, then he could try again.

In his mind he worked out a route, along the wall, across the gateway to the park, then along Frout's wall. Hanging on to bushes, gaps in the bricks, anything. He would have to be agile. *How I wish I was a monkey*, he thought.

Then he set out. Bit by bit, he edged his way over. He tried not to think about the gaping sky beneath him. Like a rock climber, he concentrated on each

foothold and each handhold that presented itself. One step at a time. Then the next. Only when he had made it across did he look back and breathe a sigh of relief. And dared to look at the machine.

Immediately he saw what he had to do. The main part was held by a cable to a hook in the wall. If he could unhook that, then something – he wasn't sure what – would happen. Maybe it would fall and then …

He reached down and twisted the cable free. With a sharp snap, the machine lurched round, swinging on one end. At the same time the towers wavered.

Cal clung on. His foot found a place by a missing brick, and his hand found a thick nail to grasp hold

of. He closed his eyes and waited. He could feel something was happening.

A moment later there was an ear-splitting noise, a noise that drilled through his bones and shook his teeth and made his eyeballs quiver. The whole of Frout's yard – the machine, the metal towers, the sheds – all began to break free and fall into the sky. They gathered momentum, rose above the houses – shrieking metal scraping and grating and clashing together.

And then, growing smaller and smaller and fainter and fainter, the further away they travelled from the earth into the sky.

The anti-gravity force had gone, pulling all the metal from Frout's yard with it. Without the force, Cal felt a familiar push towards the ground. Gravity was back. He managed to smile. *This feels better. This is as it should be*, he thought. 'Gravity: keep pushing,' he said aloud. He felt the warm sun on his back and the brick against his cheek. He tried loosening his grip, then he relaxed and opened his eyes. Gravity held him again to the wall.

'Look out!' cried Frankie, nearby.

Cal looked over. Frankie was staring into the sky. The bugs and birds were returning!

Leaping from the wall, Cal snatched Frankie up, prising his jaws from the trunk of the bush he was sheltering under. Together they scrambled over the wall into Cal's garden, and the safety of the shed. They hid inside, and listened to the *pitter-patter thump bing bang bong buzz* of things returning to earth.

After a minute or two, when it was quiet again, they peeped out and looked up, half expecting to see the towers falling back to earth. But they were far away, sucked out to space by the force field of the machine, and the sky was a beautiful empty blue.

They stumbled into the garden, sank on to the warm grass, and felt the earth pressing against their bodies.

'I am never going to move from here,' said Frankie, with feeling.

Cal looked at him and smiled with relief. Further off, Frout was wandering unsteadily around their garden. He was following a bee, buzzing from bloom to bloom.

It felt dreamlike, this return to reality. It was a beautiful summer's morning again, the air was cool and scented, birds twittered, the grass fresh. Their world was heaven again.

Suddenly Mr and Mrs Barraclough erupted out of the patio doors into the garden. They were still in their pyjamas and nightshirts, their hair on end.

'A scene of indescribable devastation,' Mrs Barraclough said, as if she was a reporter.

'A nightmare. A nightmare,' Mr Barraclough repeated. 'Have you seen our house? Destroyed! Devastated! Shaken to smithereens. Blasted to bits.'

They picked up Cal and hugged him until he could hardly breathe. 'I'm OK,' he kept saying. 'I'm OK. I just can't breathe!' Mrs Barraclough kissed Frankie's wet nose. Then they turned on their neighbour.

'Mr Frout!' hissed Mrs Barraclough, pulling herself up to her full height and snorting like a horse.

Frout turned, blinking. He seemed transfixed by a rose.

'Well?' demanded Mr Barraclough, puffing himself up like a turkey.

Frout looked at them all. They seemed to expect something of him.

'What a beautiful garden,' he said, softly.

'What?' Mr Barraclough shook with silent rage. 'Have you seen my house?' he demanded. He was practically clucking.

'Ah. Sorry,' said Frout.

'SSSSSorry?' squealed Mr Barraclough, his eyes popping out of his head.

'Dad,' said Cal quickly. 'I turned it on. It was my fault.'

His father turned to him. 'You?'

Cal nodded.

'Made that … CHAOS?' he boomed.

Cal nodded again. He decided to tell his dad the extraordinary truth. 'We've discovered the opposite of gravity. Well, *he* has,' he indicated their neighbour.

His father ran his hand across his stubble. He was a man of vision. 'There's no telling where this could end,' he said darkly. 'Without gravity, the earth would wheel away from the sun. Life itself would be extinguished!' He narrowed his eyes. 'Tell me, Mr Frout. Once science has discovered something, can you ever … *un*discover it?' He stared at Frout with a threatening glint in his eyes.

Frout nodded slowly. 'Yes, I … I … believe you could.'

'Good,' said Mr Barraclough. He had the air of a man who had struck a deal. 'Good.'

'Mind you,' said Frout, dreamily, 'I was never quite sure how it worked in the first place.'

Frout gazed around at the garden. 'This is very nice,' he said approvingly. 'Peaceful.'

He looked over at his own garden, at the space where the two towers had stood. Suddenly he knew what he was going to do.

Chapter 10

In the next six weeks Mr Frout worked on his garden. He had lorries bring in fresh soil. He ordered mature trees and a ready-made lawn. He invented an elaborate water feature – part mountain stream, part pond, where fish lurked under lily leaves and dragonflies skimmed the water.

He made a lawn with stepping stones and little pathways, with benches dotted here and there. He built a beautiful garden and he took great delight in it.

In time, he waved to Mr and Mrs Barraclough, and they waved back. It helped that he had organised extensive repairs to their house and belongings.

One day, after school, Cal and Frankie went to Mr Frout's. Frankie sat by the pond admiring the new garden.

'Beautiful,' he drawled.

They heard the gentle *snip-snip* of shears clipping a hedge.

'Hello there,' said Mr Frout, appearing with a smile from behind the fountain at the head of the mountain stream.

'Hi,' said Cal.

Frout sat on a nearby bench. He wore a wide-brimmed hat and a waistcoat, and a pair of old trousers and boots. He looked different – like a gardener – relaxed.

'I never knew,' he confided, 'that I would get so much pleasure from gardening. You know, working with nature, rather than taking it apart. I've seen some gorgeous butterflies today. And, I'm thinking I might have a wild garden for the birds over there, so they have somewhere to build nests.'

'Oh,' Cal was quiet. 'So you're not doing any more experiments?'

'Well, this is a kind of experiment. I'm experimenting with different plants, seeing how I can tame them to make a beautiful garden.'

'But you're not doing any more experiments with gravity? Or with metals? Or compressed air?'

'No. I'm all done with that. Let's just say it was too exciting.'

There was a silence.

'And anyway, I'm not sure that humans are ready for life without gravity. And birds and insects and animals certainly aren't.'

There was another silence.

'Is anything the matter?' Frout asked.

Cal screwed up his courage.

'I was wondering, do you know where I could get one of those big magnets?'

Richard Hamilton is the author of a number of picture books as well as writing young fiction for children. In conjunction with writing books, Richard works at the BBC, running its location library. He also works part-time writing and abridging stories for BBC Radio 4. He lives in London with his wife and two daughters.

Sam Hearn received a BA Hons in Illustration from Kingston University. He divides his time between working as a bookseller at the Lion and Unicorn in Richmond and illustrating children's books. This is Sam's second book for Bloomsbury.

Praise for *Violet and the Mean and Rotten Pirates* …

'Violet and the Mean and Rotten Pirates ... is a delight, and will have newly independent readers giggling from beginning to end. It's a fast furious story of an inefficent band of pirates who board a ship that has been looted already, and find nothing but a baby. So Violet, soon renamed Vile, begins an unconventional life on the "Sleek Sally", experiencing wild adventures and loads of very special love - fabulous stuff.'

Wendy Cooling

'While being full of action, this is much better than the usual, knockabout pirate stuff, with good dialogue and elegant, restrained prose ... exemplary early reading material.'

Daily Telegraph

'There's plenty of humour in this well-paced adventure tale.'

Anne Johnstone, *Glasgow Herald*

'This is packed with colloquial dialogue, which creates colourful characters and a speedy pace, and lots of lively illustrations.'

Junior Magazine

VIOLET and the MEAN and ROTTEN PIRATES

RICHARD HAMILTON

illustrated by Sam Hearn